Fancy That

Written by Esther Hershenhorn
Illustrated by Megan Lloyd

Fancy That

ALMSHOUSE

ENTER

SCHOOL

Holiday House / New York

To my sister, Judith Chairnoff Richards.
Though far, you were near, cheering me on.
Love,
E. H.

To the Kauffmans:
May your travels be merry
and your homecomings sweet.
M. L.

Text copyright © 2003 by Esther Hershenhorn
Illustrations copyright © 2003 by Megan Lloyd
All Rights Reserved
Printed in the United States of America
www.holidayhouse.com
First Edition
Library of Congress Cataloging-in-Publication Data
Hershenhorn, Esther.
Fancy that / by Esther Hershenhorn; illustrated by Megan Lloyd.— 1st ed.
p. cm.
Summary: In 1841 in Pennsylvania, Pippin Biddle,
determined to get his three orphaned sisters out of the poorhouse,
tries to earn a living as an itinerant painter.
ISBN 0-8234-1605-4 (hardcover)
[1. Artists— Fiction. 2. Brothers and sisters— Fiction.
3. Orphans— Fiction. 4. Pennsylvania— Fiction.] I. Lloyd, Megan, ill. II. Title.
PZ7.H432425 Fan 2003
E—dc21   2001039279

Berks County, Pennsylvania Almshouse, 1841

PIPPIN BIDDLE DID THE ONLY THING he could once he and his sisters were orphaned without warning. He packed up his father's paints and readied for the road.

"Be brave!" he told the sweet three. There was Emma, the oldest, and Lyddie, the littlest, and Martha, in-between. "I'll travel about and paint people's portraits, earning our keep as Father did." Pip returned their kisses. "I promise by Christmas we'll have our own home."

Pip drove the wagon forward, trunks and paint tins bumping. He patted the keepsakes tucked inside his pocket: a red ribbon from Emma, Martha's favorite pinecone, and Lyddie's treasure, the tiniest of bells.

Pip turned north. Biscuit jumped onto his lap.

In time they found the Post Road that ran beside the river. The riverbank's sweet-smelling trees were in bloom.

Pip "Hallo!"-ed heartily to those passing by, to peddlers and merchants, to other limners, too. There were teamsters and tinkers and drovers coaxing sheep. There were families on the move, their households in tow. Biscuit ran back and forth. He woofed and wagged his tail.

Night time fell. Pip knew his destination. His father had told tales of the Dutchman's Inn.

Pip promised portraits for his room and board. He toiled hard, from supper's end through sunup.

He'd watched his father work. That was all he knew of painting. So he tried his hand now. He learned to use his colors. Time and again, Pip painted Biscuit's face.

Pippin Biddle
Left-handed
Limner &
Fancy Painter
CORRECT LIKENESSES
TAKEN WITH ELEGANCE AND DISPATCH
☞ FULL FACE & SIDE VIEWS
3/4 VIEWS & FULL
☞ MONEY RETURNED IF
DISSATISFIED WITH LIKENESS
☞ ANIMAL
LIKENESS

When the new day began, Pip staked his father's signboard on the path that led to the Dutchman's Inn.

"Fancy that!" Pip declared.

His sisters had made the signboard his. Pip nuzzled Biscuit.

"Though far, they are near," he said, "cheering us on."

Spring ran her course. Sadly, men, women, and children all huffed their displeasure with Pip's finished portraits.

Was he blind as a bat, they asked, to render such likenesses?

How could he not see a fine and handsome face?

When the Dutchman himself took issue with his portrait, Pip knew he'd boot him out early in the morning.

Pip longed to see his sisters again. He worried that the three were scrubbing poorhouse floors. Emma's red ribbon was all that gave him hope.

Pip fashioned blooms and twigs around Biscuit's neck, then painted his likeness to cheer his sisters on.

At dawn Pip found a willing traveler who would trade his mare for Pip's horse and wagon. The wagon's new owner would deliver Pip's canvas.

"Be brave!" Pip wrote. "We'll have our home by Christmas!"

Pip headed west, with Biscuit in the saddle.

Pip painted doors and frames for bread and food, seven days and seven nights. In time he steered his horse through the turns of the Pike, a road Pip knew his father had traveled. Fruit trees dotted hills and dales.

Night time fell. Pip headed for the Crossing and the cooper's shop he recognized from his father's tales.

Pip painted portraits for room and board once more. Again he toiled from supper's end through sunup.

He was trying his hand now at full and partial portraits. Biscuit posed till night slipped away.

When the new day began, Pip staked his father's signboard on the road that led to the Crossing's shops.

Summer ran her course. Sadly, judges, clerks, and parsons all turned up their noses at Pip's finished portraits.

Was he missing one eye, they asked, to render such likenesses?

How could he not see a fine form and figure?

When the cooper himself took issue with his portrait, Pip knew he'd boot him out early in the morning.

The Honorable
Clerk of Courts

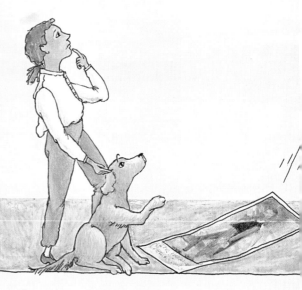

Pippin Biddle
Left-handed
Limner &
Fancy Painter
CORRECT LIKENESSES

Be brave. We'll have our home by Christmas! love, Pippin

Pip longed to be with his faraway sisters. He fretted that the three were baking poorhouse bread. Only the scent of Martha's pinecone gave Pip hope.

Pip fashioned berries around Biscuit's neck, then painted his likeness once again to cheer his sisters.

At dawn Pip found yet another traveler, who would trade his handcart for Pip's horse and bags. The horse's new owner would deliver the canvas, so Pip wrote the message he'd sent once before.

Pip headed south, with Biscuit as his scout.

Weeks went by while Pip painted doors or lent a hand at harvesting to feed himself and Biscuit. Once on the Gap Road, Biscuit gathered leaves. Every tree flaunted autumn hues.

Night time fell. Pip headed
for the friends' farms he knew so
well from his father's tales.

One day's work brought one
night's stay. Again Pip toiled from
supper's end through sunup.

Now he would try his hand at full
family portraits. Such large canvases
would surely bring grand sums. Biscuit
posed with his newfound friends.

When the new day began, Pip posted his handbills on roadside trees and farmers' fences.

Fall nudged winter. Sadly, mothers, fathers, and sons all spat their disapproval of Pip's finished portraits.

Was he blinded at birth, they asked, to render such likenesses?

How could he not see fine kith and kin?

When the farmer's family took issue with their portrait, Pip knew they'd boot him out early in the morning.

Be Brave! We'll have our home by Christmas! love, Pippin

Pip longed to hear his sisters again. He feared they were in the woods seeking poorhouse kindling. Only the ping of Lyddie's bell gave Pip hope.

Pip fashioned leaves and keepsakes round Biscuit's neck, then painted his likeness to cheer the sisters on.

Dawn brought a cobbler who was traveling for Thanksgiving. He traded warm boots for Pip's handcart. He bundled the canvas to take to Pip's sisters once Pip wrote the same words he'd written them before.

Pip walked east, with Biscuit at his side.

The two trudged through snowdrifts on unknown roads. The wind's shrill whistle was the only sound for miles.

Young Pip wept at the sight of families gathered.

When, Pip wondered, would his family do the same?

One last time Pip painted a portrait, rendering the likenesses he knew so well. Pip carried Biscuit and the painted canvas on through the storm, a painter no more.

The snowy road led to the poorhouse. Spruce and pine wore their holiday garb.

Pretty things hung on neighbors' doors. Pretty things Pip had never seen before.

"Fancy that!" Pip declared. He read aloud a cabin's sign, HOME OF THE BIDDLES.

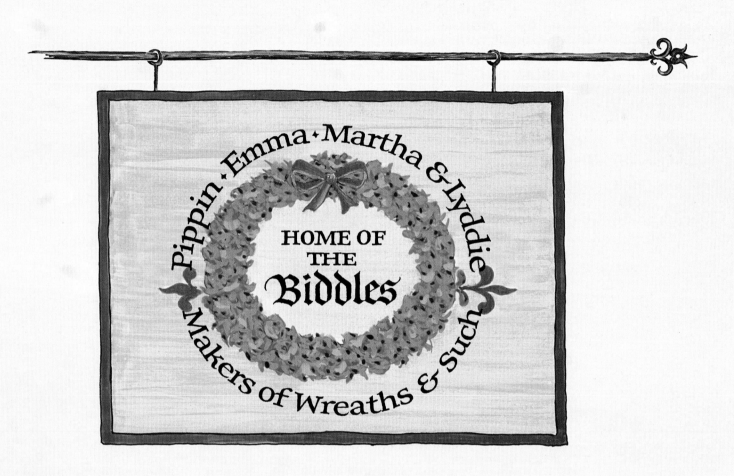

Pippin • Emma • Martha & Lyddie

HOME OF
THE
Biddles

Makers of Wreaths & Such

For all these seasons his sisters had been working, and
weaving, with leaves and such, Christmas wreaths to sell.

"Though far, you were near," they told Pip, "cheering us on."
It was Christmas. They were home.
Fancy that, indeed.

AUTHOR'S NOTE

Before the camera was invented in the late 1840s, artists traveled about America capturing people's lives and likenesses on canvas. Known as limners— or fancy painters when they painted signs and surfaces— these portrait painters moved about the countryside, setting up their studios in inns, shops, homes, and farmhouses. Many limners were self-taught. Often, they posed their subjects against prepared backgrounds, as if by formula. Then they rendered their subjects in a simple, flat style, using oils, egg tempera, watercolors, or pen and ink. Some limners specialized in subject matter, painting only animals or sailing vessels, buildings or landscapes. Today, people consider the discovered works of America's limners and fancy painters folk art and treasure the paintings accordingly. Many of these paintings, often unsigned, hang in museums around the world.

Pippin Biddle
Left-handed Limner & Fancy Painter

CORRECT LIKENESSES
TAKEN WITH ELEGANCE AND DISPATCH
☞ FULL FACE & SIDE VIEWS
3/4 VIEWS & FULL
☞ MONEY RETURNED IF
DISSATISFIED WITH LIKENESS
☞ ANIMAL
LIKENESSES

ARTIST'S NOTE

The illustrations in this book were done primarily in pen, ink, and egg tempera. Egg tempera is a very old medium, predating the use of oil paints. I chose this medium in order to capture the flatter style of nineteenth-century itinerant limners. To make egg tempera I begin by grinding raw color pigments on a slab of marble with a glass grinder known as a muller. I add distilled water to the pigments to make a paste. I store the pigment pastes in small glass jars, where they will keep for many months.

When I am ready to paint, I collect a fresh egg from one of my chickens, break the shell, and separate the yolk from the white. I hold the yolk in my cupped hand and pierce it with the tip of the knife. The yolk drains into a small jar under my hand, and I give the yolk membrane to one of my cats as a treat! Then I mix one teaspoon of water into the yolk to make my egg tempera medium.

I'm almost ready to paint, but first I have to mix a small dollop of pigment paste with an equal amount of egg tempera medium. This creates the egg tempera paint! I mix up only the colors I will use in one day of painting because egg tempera paint does not keep well. I have to start with fresh paint each day.

Egg tempera takes a bit of time to prepare and use, but it is a medium that lends itself to crisp detail and color. I can build up many subtle layers of tempera, called glazing, which gives me a great deal of control over my painting. I really enjoyed using this very old medium to create the illustrations in *Fancy That*.